For Constantin - ST
For Ellen - HS

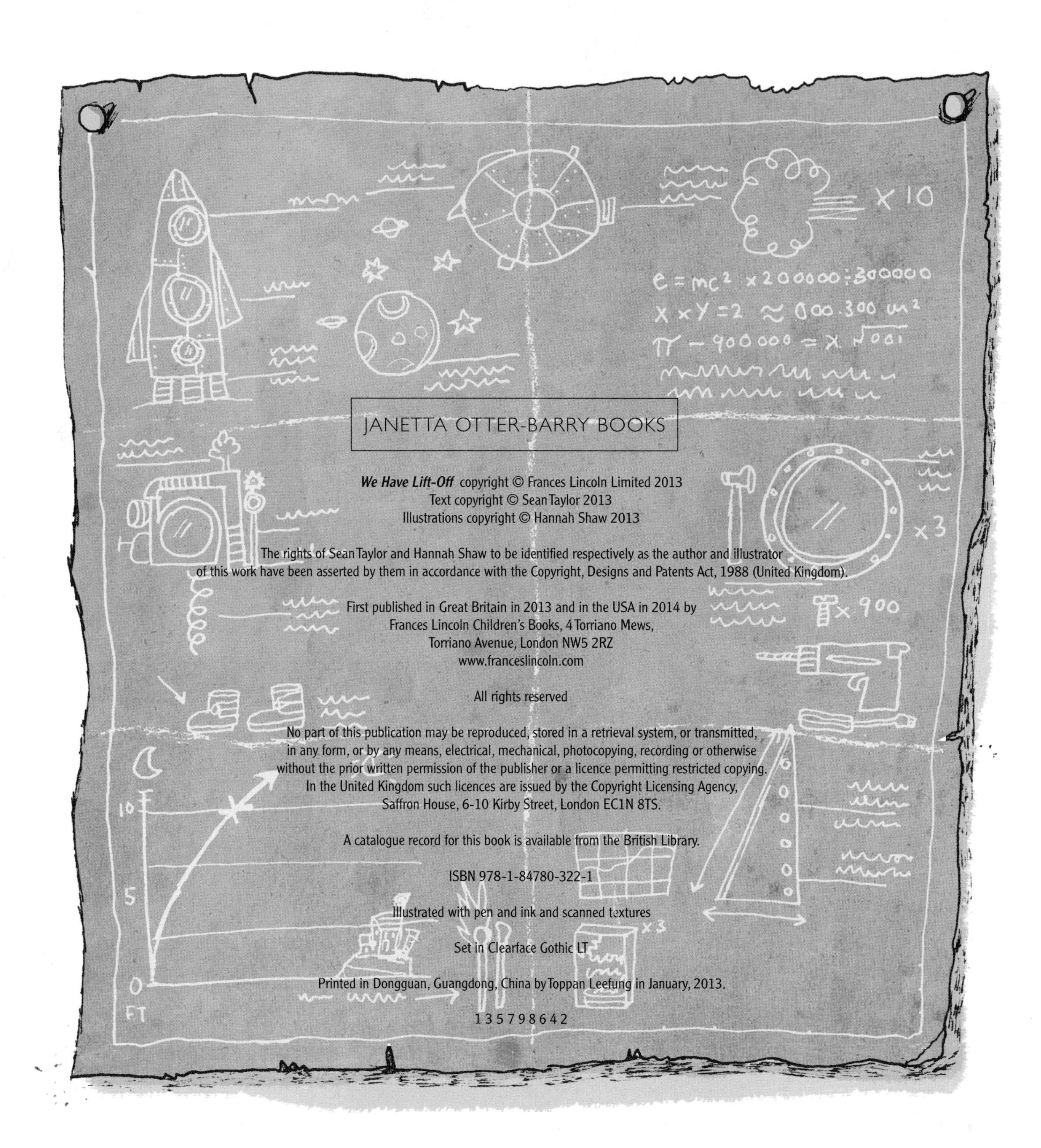

JANETTA OTTER-BARRY BOOKS

First published in Great Britain in 2013 and in the USA in 2014 by
Frances Lincoln Children's Books, 4 Torriano Mews,
Torriano Avenue, London NW5 2RZ
www.franceslincoln.com

A catalogue record for this book is available from the British Library.

ISBN 978-1-84780-322-1

Illustrated with pen and ink and scanned textures

Set in Clearface Gothic LT

Printed in Dongguan, Guangdong, China by Toppan Leefung in January, 2013.

1 3 5 7 9 8 6 4 2

WE HAVE LIFT-OFF!

Sean Taylor

Illustrated by
Hannah Shaw

F
FRANCES LINCOLN
CHILDREN'S BOOKS

You're looking at the first chicken in outer space, **which was me.**

You see, I used to live on Mr Tanner's Farm. And it really was a RIGHT OLD DUMP.

Mr Tanner poisoned
the air with smoke. . .

and filled the
river with junk. . .

and cut down
all the trees. . .

and crammed us animals
into a crumbling barn.

But his house just kept getting BIGGER

and **BIGGER**

and **BIGGER!**

We animals couldn't take it any more.

So we held a meeting in a top-secret location, to see if there was anything we could do.

And we decided to do something...

We built an intergalactic rocket so that we could escape, away from Mr Tanner, and up to the CLEAR, CLEAN STARS.

It was a difficult plan. But if it worked, we were sure that news would spread. Then ANIMALS ALL ROUND THE WORLD would start doing THE SAME THING!

Because, let's face it, animals have had enough of trying to share our planet with ***people.***

People just keep on
MESSING THINGS UP.
TO THE MOON...

The pig who designed our rocket reckoned it was strong enough to carry us all. But he said someone had go on a **TEST FLIGHT.**

And that was when I got chosen!

I was given moonboots, a space helmet and a map. And a supply of **cornflakes** that looked enough to last for a whole life.

I was shown the START button (which I was supposed to press at the start).

And the EMERGENCY ABANDON MISSION button (which I wasn't supposed to press, except in an emergency).

Then,

5 - 4 - 3 - 2 - 1......

WE HAVE LIFT-OFF!

Up I went... away from the litter and clutter of Mr Tanner's farm!

First of all, everything went fine.

I was in radio contact
with the Flight Director at
ANIMAL MISSION CONTROL.
And I was ON MY WAY
TO THE **STARS!**

But there was a problem.

I was holding the map
upside-*down*.

And suddenly the rocket was heading
back towards our planet.

"DON'T COME BACK!" said the Flight Director.
But it was too late. The rocket was the wrong way round, and the only way was down.
ROCKET CAM

We had to do another TEST FLIGHT and this time a very clever rabbit was chosen.

He put on moonboots and a space helmet.

He was given a map and a big box of carrots.

Then,
5 – 4 – 3 – 2 – 1.....
WE HAVE LIFT-OFF!
Up went the rabbit...
out of the smog and smoke
of Mr Tanner's farm!

First of all everything went fine.
The rabbit was ON HIS WAY
TO THE **STARS**!

Then there was a problem.

I think the rabbit got nervous.

He started eating carrots
very fast. . .

and the box got stuck over his head.
He bumped the steering wheel
and the rocket started
heading back.
"DON'T COME BACK!"
said the Flight Director.
But it was too late.
The rabbit couldn't get the box off,
and the only way was
down.

We still had to do a successful TEST FLIGHT, and a very calm sheep was chosen next.

She was given moonboots, a space helmet, a map and a supply of cabbage leaves in LITTLE boxes that she couldn't get stuck over her head.

Then,

5 - 4 - 3 - 2 - 1.....

WE HAVE LIFT-OFF!

Up went the sheep...
away from the muck and
junk of Mr Tanner's farm!

First of all, everything went fine. The sheep was ON HER WAY TO THE **STARS**!

Then there was a problem.

The sheep fell asleep. What's worse, she leant her head on the EMERGENCY ABANDON MISSION button so the rocket turned automatically back.

"For Goodness' sake!" said the Flight Director. **"DON'T COME BACK!"**

But it was **too late.**

The sheep was asleep,

and the only way **was down.**

And that was when Mr Tanner came
to find out what the noise was about.

But the joke was on him, because somehow he pressed the START button.

Then,

5 – 4 – 3 – 2 – 1......

WE HAVE LIFT-OFF!

Up went Mr Tanner... ON HIS WAY TO THE STARS.

And we never saw him again!

It wasn't what we'd planned.
But actually it was better than
trying to escape in the rocket.

And news has spread.

Now ANIMALS ALL ROUND THE WORLD
are building intergalactic rockets and sending
people like Mr Tanner up to the stars.

So if you're one of the people who makes
a mess of our planet... **WATCH OUT!**

It could be **your** turn next!